BIGGER BITES FOR
CHOMPS
BIGGER READERS!

The Boy Who Would Live Forever

Daniel knows he can never

think of the future.

His destiny is to stay the same forever.

He doesn't know why.

He doesn't even know who he is.

What has he done to deserve this?

MORE CHOMPS TO SINK YOUR TEETH INTO!

STELLA BY THE SEA
Ruth Starke

COMING IN FALL 2006

THE TWILIGHT GHOST
Colin Thiele

WALTER WANTS TO BE A WEREWOLF
Richard Harland

CHOMPS
BIGGER BITES FOR BIGGER READERS!

The Boy Who Would Live Forever

Is Daniel destined to be 12-years-old *forever*?

Moya Simons

RUNNING PRESS
KIDS
PHILADELPHIA·LONDON

For Jules, the eternal boy

9   8   7   6   5   4   3   2   1
Digit on the right indicates the number of this printing

Library of Congress Control Number: 2005905019

ISBN-13: 978-0-7624-2624-9
ISBN-10: 0-7624-2624-1

Original design by David Altheim, Penguin Design Studio.
Additional design for this edition by Frances J. Soo Ping Chow

Typography: ITC Berkeley, MetaPlus, and New Century Schoolbook

This book may be ordered by mail from the publisher.
Please include $2.50 for postage and handling.
But try your bookstore first!

This edition published by Running Press Kids, an imprint of
Running Press Book Publishers
125 South Twenty-second Street
Philadelphia, Pennsylvania 19103-4399

Visit us on the web!
www.runningpress.com

Ages 8–12
Grades 3–6

Chapter

Once, a long time ago, a boy ran, stumbling at times, across a Scottish meadow. He had reddish-brown hair and piercing blue eyes that were wide with fear.

The boy had no idea where he was. For that matter, he had no idea who he was. There were pictures dancing in his mind of twin suns and silver figures with outstretched arms.

He scratched himself on thorns as he climbed over a hedge, then stopped beside a tree and sat down on the grass. Where was he? Who was he?

What was he to do? He clutched his hands, and stared at them as though he'd never seen hands before. He wriggled his fingers, curiously touching the small pinpoints of blood on them from where he'd cut himself.

He heard a noise and turned around. A man, riding a horse, was galloping towards him. The boy was frightened. The horse was so big and the man's face seemed angry.

They stopped beside him. The boy could feel the hot breath of the horse. He stood up stiffly and leaned against the tree. What was he to do?

"What are ye doing on my land?" The man squinted down at him.

The boy couldn't answer. He understood what the farmer was saying though the words were just odd sounds. The question the man asked him took the form of a picture in his mind.

The man hesitated. He climbed off the horse

and stared hard at the boy. "Ye be a small lad," he said. Noting the terror in the boy's eyes, he added, "Don't be afeared. I haven't come to harm ye."

He took him home. The boy sat in front of the man on the horse. The wind whipped his face and his body jerked up and down. The boy was confused but not frightened now. He felt the kindness in the man and the gentle nature of the horse.

The farm house had a thatched roof and whitewashed walls. A rose vine trailed around the door and small windows. The farmer's wife wiped her hands on her apron, curiously eyed the boy, and said to her husband, "How come ye be bringing home a lad? Where's he from?"

She sat the boy at a wooden table and gave him a steaming bowl of soup and crusty bread, then sat with him near the fireplace and wrapped a blanket around him. He read in her mind that she didn't have children. Children? A picture formed in his mind. *Ah yes, small ones like me, he thought.*

"He be lost," said the farmer. "His mind is foggy. He don't seem to know who he is. Someone must be out looking for the lad."

"Look at the cuts on his hands," said the wife, and she held out his thin hands. "Someone's been treating him ill."

"It just be scratches," said the farmer. "Tis nothing."

"Oh, but he's got such blue eyes," his wife said. "And, look, dimples in those skinny cheeks."

That night the boy slept in a warm bed. The farmer's wife tucked him in and pushed his red-brown hair from his face.

"Have ye no idea where ye come from?" she asked him as she smoothed his hair.

He worked hard to form words on his lips.

"No," he said, rolling the sounds in his mouth like unfamiliar food. "I can't remember."

The next day the farmer asked around the nearby village. No one knew anything about the child.

"It's as if he be sent to us," said his wife and she clasped her hands together and smiled. "I want to keep him. We will call him Daniel."

"Hush," said the farmer, and he put a warning finger over his lip as if someone else was listening. "The lad's not ours."

But no one claimed Daniel. He stayed on at the farm. The farmer's wife taught him to read and write. He made friends with children from the village nearby. They climbed hedges and picked blackberries in the forest. Slowly the friends grew taller and older. Daniel didn't. He always looked and acted as if he were eleven or twelve years of age.

The children in the village made fun of him. "Ye be a tiny, skinny runt," they said to him.

"I am not," he replied. He ended up fighting, always coming off the worst because he was smaller.

Time went by. The farmer and his wife grew older, but Daniel didn't. His face stayed young and he didn't grow taller. His arms and legs were thin, gangly and child-like and, though he was smart and could read and write well, he had the mind of a child.

His friends did not stay friends. They grew older and had different interests. They no longer leapt over country hedges or came home with their mouths black from eating berries in the forest. Some went to work in the coal mines. Others became blacksmiths and cobblers or remained on the family farm. Daniel stayed just as he'd always been. A child of about eleven or twelve years of age, who helped his father plant crops; who cut and stacked hay for the farm animals. Who pretended he was a pirate and put a patch over one eye and climbed trees.

"He's got some disease," people whispered to one another in the village. The more superstitious ones said, "He's bewitched." And others said jealously, "He's got the secret of eternal youth. Why him and not us?"

Eventually the farmer and his wife stopped Daniel from leaving the farm.

"They think ye have magic powers," said the farmer. He stared at Daniel and shook his head. "Ye be twenty-five years now, Daniel. Tis not natural that ye stay a wee lad. It's best you stay away from people."

"I can make them like me," said Daniel. He'd discovered that he could burrow into minds. Rearrange thoughts.

"There's too many, lad," said the farmer. He'd noticed that Daniel had a way of confusing people who asked him too many questions. "Besides, ye cannot go round messing with everyone's thoughts. Tis wrong."

The farmer's wife died that year. Daniel helped the farmer bury her at the top of the hill. He stood beside the farmer, his eyes streaming with tears.

The farmer said to Daniel, "It seems to me that ye'll never grow old, Daniel. I don't know why, but it must be something to do with where ye came from. I'm old now and when my time comes, ye must move and find another family to live with, but beware. Everyone wants to live forever, and when people discover that ye don't grow old like they do they'll want to know your secret. When time passes and ye don't get any bigger and ye see the stares, then it's time to move on. Ye are not to be pulled apart by fancy scientists so they can work out why ye stay young. Ye must remember that."

"But, father, I don't know why I don't grow old," said Daniel. "I don't want to stay a child forever. I want to grow up."

"I know, I know," said the farmer. His face became thoughtful and Daniel looked sadly at the pouches and wrinkles under his father's eyes. He noticed the way his back was stooped and how his father sometimes forgot what day it was.

The years rolled by, and one day his father did not wake up in the morning, though Daniel shook the farmer's thin shoulders and tried to open his closed eyes. Why did people grow old and die, he wondered? Why didn't *he* grow old?

He buried the farmer on the hill next to his wife. "Tis a peaceful spot," he said to him. He wiped tears away from his face. "I'll be moving on then."

He didn't know what to do with the farm animals. He opened the latch on the gate of the hen yard and set the hens free. He opened the gate to the paddock where two goats and a cow grazed.

"Goodbye," he whispered. "Goodbye."

Daniel took money from the box behind his father's desk and walked up the lane leading from the farm. He was a thirty-year-old man who looked only twelve. What would he do? Where would he go? London. He would head for London.

The year was 1815.

Chapter  2

"I found him at the train station, sleeping on the bench beside the platform," the woman said.

The policeman leaned across the counter and scratched his chin. "What's your name, kid?"

"Daniel." He stared up at the policeman.

"And your surname?"

"I don't remember."

"Where do you live? Do you remember that?"

"No, I just remember being woken up by this lady here at the train station. I don't know how I got there." Daniel wriggled in the heavy wooden chair and stared up at the policeman through innocent blue eyes.

The policeman said, "Are you sure now? Maybe you've had a fight with Mom and Dad. Is that it?"

"No," said Daniel carefully. How many times over the years had he said this? "I just don't remember how I got here. My head hurts."

Daniel put his hand to the side of his head and made a face. "Ouch."

"He's lost his memory," said the lady. "I've already asked him questions, officer, and I think you should get him to a hospital. Someone, somewhere must be looking for him."

The police officer suggested they sit in the waiting room while he made calls. Another policeman came in and took a photograph of Daniel.

"It's to help identify you," he said, "though we've received no reports of a kid missing in this suburb. Still, you were found at a train station. We'll send this photo throughout the state. Throughout the country if we have to. Don't worry. Your parents will come and pick you up and this will soon just be a bad dream."

Daniel concentrated hard as the policeman took the photo. At the moment the camera flashed, his features changed. The red-brown hair darkened, the nose lengthened, the piercing blue eyes became wide and rounded. When the picture was sent around the different police stations, it wouldn't look like Daniel at all.

He was taken to a hospital. The lady who had found him came along. "I'm Sally Davis," she said. "I'll stay with you until you've been sorted out. Don't worry."

Sally was tall with curly dark hair and large dark eyes. She wore a scarf around her neck and a thick red coat. She fished in her bag. "Here," she said. "Have a candy."

Daniel put a soft red sweet in his mouth. "It's sugar-free," Sally said smiling. "I'm dieting."

He sucked the candy, wishing as he'd wished a thousand times that he'd stopped ageing at the age of twenty or twenty-five rather than at twelve. Not at an age when he still looked like a kid, still felt like a kid and where people felt responsible for him.

The doctor at the hospital arranged for a lot of tests. "We're going to take a photo of the inside of your head, Daniel," he said. "It's to check whether you've hurt yourself there. My guess is, though there's no bump there, that you've probably had a knock on your head. It's caused a bit of swelling inside your brain, in that part where your memory works. As the swelling goes down, your memory will come back."

Daniel nodded. The doctors poked and prodded and, when they did a scan of his brain, he was careful to fix the pictures so that they wouldn't see anything unusual.

It was a busy hospital with nurses rushing everywhere. Sally sat with him through all the tests. "Thanks," he said to her. He noticed that she occasionally glanced at her watch. "Do you have to go to work?"

"It's okay, Daniel," she said to him. "I've phoned my boss and said I'll be late. The Department of Community Services is going to arrange for you to go to a special place they have for kids."

"Can't I go home with you?" Daniel asked. He didn't want to go to one of those homes. They were like halfway houses, where kids stayed until they were placed in foster homes. He'd been to three in the last fifteen years. The kids there hadn't liked him. Most kids didn't like him. He was . . . different.

"Um, well, well . . ." Sally twisted the ends of her scarf. "I don't know. I guess it depends on what the doctor says and the social worker the department's sending along."

He looked into her mind. She was hesitating because she knew nothing about him. She had a child, a girl. He couldn't see a husband. Yes, now he could, but he was a long way away. Divorced. Yes, she was divorced. He'd never stayed with anyone who had a child before. Somehow, children worked out quickly that he was odd and made fun of him. But there was something about Sally. Something warm and comforting about her smile.

A social worker came to the hospital. He was a youngish man, thin with wispy brown hair, called John. "I've got the results of all your tests from the doctor," he said to Daniel. "You're fine. I'm sure your memory will come back in a day or two."

"Can I go home with *her*?" Daniel pointed to

Sally. "Please."

"No, that's not allowed," John said.

Daniel was about to nudge his mind when Sally said, "Can't he come with me while you're sorting this out? I've got a child of my own." She laughed and Daniel sensed she was sorry she'd been hesitant earlier on about taking him. "I can get a hundred friends to vouch that I'm not about to kidnap Daniel."

"The hospital wants to keep him in here for observation for a day or two. Maybe I can rush this through court," said the social worker. "It really would be better for Daniel to stay with a trusted family while we locate his parents. I'll need information about you . . ."

A nurse took Daniel to the children's ward. He was given pajamas. They had a Micky Mouse design on them. He got changed and lay in his bed, his hands under the back of his head. Daniel stared around at the other children. At a boy with his leg in a cast and at another boy with a bandage around his head.

"What's wrong with you?" asked the boy with the broken leg.

"I'm just staying here for a night or two," Daniel replied. "I've lost my memory. They want to make sure I'm okay."

"You've lost your memory? Wow. So, don't you know who you are?"

"No," said Daniel.

I really don't.

Chapter

Daniel shut his eyes. His closed lids twitched while he thought about himself. After all this time—more than two hundred years—he still did not know who he really was. Even though he'd done so many things, and could unzip and rearrange the thoughts of others, he still felt like a kid. Stunted like his body at the age of twelve.

He thought back.

After he left the farm in 1815, he made his way to London. Daniel wanted to get as far away from the farm as possible and, besides, he'd heard that London was a huge city. An exciting place. He had money in his pocket and felt enthusiastic. He'd probably find work there. Daniel could read and write well. Maybe he could work in a big factory. Lots of children worked in factories. He could stay for a while until they began to look at him in that strange way that people did. If he lived carefully, by then he'd have a lot of money saved. He could move to the country, maybe find another family.

So, feeling optimistic, he climbed up onto a coach from the outskirts of his village.

"I'm going to my aunt in London," he said to the driver.

"That be a big trip and costly," said the driver, eyes glinting. He took from Daniel's hand double what the journey would normally have cost.

Daniel travelled in the small coach to Edinburgh where he and the other passengers stayed in a shabby inn, then caught a four-horse coach to London. It took over two weeks for the coach to arrive. Along the way they stopped to change the tired horses for fresh ones, to eat at small inns and to sleep for the night.

He was sometimes questioned about travelling alone. "I'm an orphan," he said quietly. "I'm travelling to London to be with my aunt."

People nodded. One lady put an arm around him. One slipped him a candy. Daniel hardly noticed the kindness. He was thinking. Would he be able to manage? He had just a little money and the whole of eternity stretched in an uneven path in front of him.

He sat in the bumpy coach on his way to London, squashed between six people, one a woman adjusting her bonnet and high-collared dress. When a mouse crawled near his shoe he quietly picked it up. While the lady looked out of the window he put the mouse in her lap.

"Ahh," she screamed when the mouse began to nibble at her arm. Daniel smiled smugly and turned the other way. For he was just a boy with the cheeky mind of a boy.

Daniel couldn't find work in London though he went from shop to shop and from factory to factory. The streets, bleak and ugly, were filled with homeless people. This was nothing like he'd expected. Nothing like the London he'd read about in books with pictures of fine men with top hats and ladies in long beautiful dresses. The little money he had left was stolen by a pickpocket in the market streets. He ended up begging for food and sleeping on a step in an alley at night.

One day he stole two loaves of bread from a baker's shop and was caught. The baker twisted his ear and turned him over to the police. Seven years they gave him. Seven years' transportation to Australia. At the time Daniel hardly cared. Anything would be better than living on the streets of London. For once, he'd been treated as an adult. Been sentenced as one and transported in a smelly hell-hole of a ship to a place called Sydney Cove.

How could people living now understand the conditions of life aboard a convict ship? How could Daniel explain what it felt like to be half-starved because the ship's owner had cut down on rations so he'd make more money on the voyage? How could you explain to someone who showered every day how he felt about spending most of the voyage under deck chained to another convict and just coming up on deck for exercise and the occasional wash?

Once, Daniel had tried to improve his conditions. He sent a thought to the ship's cook to give him extra rations, but Daniel choked on the food as the other convicts stared with anger at him. He couldn't do it again. No, he'd live like them. Suffer with them. It would end one day.

Daniel would never forget the smell of all those grimy bodies below deck. And how could he forget Ned, the ten-year-old who slept on the threadbare hammock beside him? Dear Ned, long gone. Ned, transported for stealing eggs. "Wake up, Ned," Daniel had said one morning and the chains that linked them had rattled like bones. He'd shaken Ned and vainly implored him to *please, please wake up.*

Daniel had been on deck washing himself down with other convicts when he saw the coast of New South Wales. A faint smudge on the horizon.

Someone had called out, "Land ho."

Sydney Cove. Bright with sunlight and abuzz

with sailing ships. In the distance, trees. Not the green of Scotland or England but a dusty green that spoke of glittering heat and burnt soil.

The authorities there had found him work immediately. There was work for everyone in the new colony. Good! Anything was better than being on that ship.

He'd slept at night in the jail and worked stacking boxes in a warehouse on the docks in Sydney, and Joe, the manager, felt sorry for him. Daniel had looked into him and seen a wish for a son. So he nudged his mind. Put a thought there. No one noticed that Daniel didn't go back to the jail one night.

Joe took Daniel into his home and treated Daniel well until four years passed, then five, then six.

"You don't get older," Joe said to Daniel as he helped him unload cargo from ships. "I thought by now you'd be big and strong and able to carry an elephant. You can't carry anything but the lightest cargo. You're still the same child I took home all those years ago." Joe wiped glistening beads of sweat from his brow. He frowned, then asked him, "Tell me the truth, Daniel. I want the absolute truth. How old are you?"

Daniel hesitated, then said nervously, "I'm about thirty-six."

The man looked startled, as though someone had punched him. He rubbed his forehead and was silent. Finally he said, "I will take you to see my priest."

He took Daniel to the church. The priest there raised his eyebrows in surprise. "This is a boy. He can't be thirty-six." Joe brought witnesses. One had known Daniel on the streets of London many years ago. "He was a child then," the man said. "Stealing food from barrows and shops. We were transported to Sydney Cove on the same rotting ship. He's not altered."

The priest turned pale. "You are cursed," he said to Daniel and he pointed a long skinny finger at him. "Cursed to wander the earth forever."

By then, Joe had grown old and cranky. "I wouldn't call it a curse," he said to Daniel later when they sat down to eat. "It isn't fair that I am a wrinkled old man and you are to stay a lad of twelve forever. It isn't fair." He leaned forward and clipped Daniel behind his ear.

Daniel jumped. He saw something in Joe's face that reminded him of the warning the farmer had given him.

The next day he left.

The years rolled by like waves on a beach. Each surge of tide was another passage of time. A passage of time where he met new families with whom he could stay for a while. Meantime, the world was changing. Daniel had come from an age where there was no electricity, no cars, no phones and no movies. Where people lived short lives and died of illnesses barely understood. He'd moved on to an age of amazing technology, where scientists knew how to harness nature, how to send rocket ships to the moon. A time where cars, movies and electricity were taken for granted and where medical science was so advanced that most of the old illnesses could now be treated.

He'd lived with people he called parents, only to move on when they stared and talked softly between themselves and wondered. Yes, he could have nudged them, forced them to keep him, but where did it end? There were always others in the neighborhood who noticed that he never grew older, who wanted to know his secret.

Now he lay in a hospital, his eyes shut tightly

while he thought about Sally. He would go home with her. But she had a child already. Would there be resentment? It was always safer to stay with an older couple.

He'd been with Grandma Bessie for a year. He hadn't needed to nudge her mind at all.

He was walking down the street when he saw an old lady. She had a sun hat with a huge flower in it and was bending over her plants, talking to them. He stopped and smiled at her.

Her face was thin and wrinkled and her hair was white and fluffy. He'd never seen anyone quite that old though he realized straight away that she was younger than him. Much younger. About a hundred and fifty years younger.

"Want some lemonade, Sammy?" She looked up from her flowers and smiled at him.

Daniel went inside. She made him lemonade then poured cherry flavoring in it. She sat down and said to him, "I'm glad you're back, Sammy. I've missed you. I've left your room just as it was."

She was convinced he was her son, Sammy, so he stayed. She told the neighbors that Sammy had come home.

"Isn't it wonderful," she said, and she showed the neighbors a photo of her grown-up son.

"You see I told you he'd come home one day."

"I'm her grandson," Daniel said to the neighbors later. "She's got me mixed up."

He stayed all year. She didn't mind that he didn't go to school. The neighbors worked and didn't notice. Daniel helped Grandma dig out weeds and he fetched her shopping. He watched TV with her, read old, peeling books from the bookshelf, and diced vegetables for dinner. She ruffled his hair and said, "It's grand that you're back again, Sammy."

But one day the real Sammy phoned. He was in

England and planning to come back to Australia. He was going to move in with Grandma. He, the wife and the kids.

"Goodness me," said Grandma when she got off the phone. "I'm very confused. He says he's Sammy but my Sammy's just ten-years-old. If he's telling the truth and he is Sammy, then who are you?"

Daniel left the next day. He'd miss her, the loving smile, the hot biscuits, the cherry lemonade, the jasmine-trailed fence. He'd miss the creaking swing in the back garden and the shelf in the living room with the old books.

Daniel took the pocket money she'd given him each week and went to the train station. He caught a train and got out at a station called Sunnyvale for no other reason than he was miserable and he liked the sound of the name.

It was here that Sally had found him.

Chapter 4

He went home with Sally after spending two days in the hospital.

"I'm sure that we'll locate your parents," Sally said to him brightly as she opened the car door for him. "In the meantime you can go to school with Holly. You look about her age. She's in Grade Six."

Sally lived in a small white house with no fence and a border of brightly colored flowers lining each side of the pathway like tiny soldiers.

She parked the car in the driveway. "Here," she said to Daniel, "help me carry the groceries."

He carried tall bags of cereal and bread into the house. There was a wind chime outside the front door playing a tinkling melody.

"Holly will be coming straight home after school," Sally said.

She put the groceries on a table in the kitchen. Daniel saw yellow curtains, potted plants by the window and bright fridge magnets holding up pictures of Holly. Holly as a fat baby. Holly beginning school. Holly now.

"Come, Daniel, I'll show you your room."

She showed Daniel into a small bedroom. More yellow curtains. A bed with a bedspread. On the bedspread, a picture of a car. Boy stuff, she'd think, though she'd never guess that Daniel preferred pictures of coaches and horses. He smiled at her. She'd gone through the trouble even though, as far as she knew, his parents could come any time and get him.

"Great," he said.

Sally reached down and hugged him. There was that old feeling inside of him—a mixture of wanting to be part of a family forever and knowing that it couldn't last.

"I've got to go back to work. I work down the road in a pet shop," said Sally. "Holly will be home from school in about an hour. Are you okay? Any headaches? Any memories coming back?"

"No." Daniel shook his head.

Sally left him sitting on a purple beanbag in front of the TV, watching a spy movie.

He heard the latch in the door open. Nervously, he stood up.

He heard the sounds of shoes padding down the hallway.

"I'm Holly," the dark-haired girl said as she walked into the living room.

She was a little taller than him, with large dark

eyes. He noticed with some surprise that she didn't have eyelashes. He wasn't actually sure about her eyebrows. Either they were very light or had been pencilled in. It didn't make her look unattractive though. Holly's eyes filled her whole face. She had pink cheeks and a wide smile. Her hair was straight and shoulder-length.

"I'm Daniel," said Daniel. He shifted uncomfortably from foot to foot.

"Mom told me all about you. About how you've lost your memory and you're staying with us until your parents show up. It must be creepy not to know who you are."

Daniel nodded.

She sat in a chair and, because he stood awkwardly beside her, she gestured to him, "Sit down. Do I make you uptight? I don't mean to. Don't you remember anything?"

I remember all my families. The kind ones and the

not so kind. I remember the days that I left my families and put thoughts in their minds so they wouldn't come looking for me. I remember everything except how I came to be different.

"No," he said. "I don't remember anything."

"Oh, well, don't worry. Mom's cool. You'll be fine here. Come on, smile. You look miserable. You can come to school with me until your parents find you."

She flicked her dark hair back from her face. "That's an awful video you're watching. That spy's a triple-agent. In the end, even he's not sure who he's working for."

Daniel laughed. He'd never had a sister. A sister. He tasted the new word. It might work out. Another child in his home. For a few years until they noticed, anyway. He could put a thought in Sally's mind to keep him here. He'd have to go to school again. Yuck. He knew sixth grade back to front and inside out.

Later, Sally came home. She sat at the computer, which was tucked away in a corner of the living room.

"I'm writing an e-mail to Nanna," she called out to Holly.

"Want to come for a walk, Daniel?" said Holly. "I can show you the neighborhood. Not that it's very fascinating, but maybe you'll see something that might jog your memory."

"Go," Sally called out. "Just don't be gone too long."

He and Holly walked up the road. Past lots of small houses with neat gardens. "There's the school." Holly pointed to a big school yard. In the middle of it were dark red-brick buildings.

"Are the kids okay?"

"It's like any other school, silly. Some of the kids are painful and some are fine. You'll probably be in my class. You look about my age. Do you remember how old you are?"

"Um, eleven or twelve," said Daniel. *And next year I'll be eleven or twelve, and the year after that, and forever more.*

"How long has your dad been living away from you," he asked, kicking a small stone along the pathway.

"How'd you know that?" Holly asked.

"Well, I sort of guessed it. There were only pictures of you and your mom on the fridge."

"He's been gone for ages, and I don't know how you guessed it. How can you work out something like that and not remember anything about yourself?"

"Yeah, it's nuts," Daniel agreed. "Maybe I'm a kid-detective who got knocked on the head by a hitman. Any time now my memory will come back and I'll tell you about my life as a kid-cop."

Holly giggled. She told him about herself, about the friend she had at school. He gently nudged her mind. She was troubled about something.

"Now, it's your turn. What can you remember?" she asked him. "You must remember something. I mean, you remember how to speak, and you remember your first name is Daniel. What else do you remember?"

Daniel hesitated. "Nothing," he said finally. He shrugged and put his hands in his pockets. "Just your mom turning up at the train station. What if my parents don't look for me? Do you think your mother would mind me staying?"

"Staying? You mean, living with us? Oh well, that's not going to happen. Of course your parents will turn up. And you're going to get your memory back any time. Maybe I should give you a big thump on your head. I've heard that works sometimes."

She laughed. Her teeth were white and shiny. The wind blew the hair back from her face. It was strange how she didn't have eyelashes, not even a single one, and when he looked closely he could see that her eyebrows were pencilled in. He'd like to ask her about that. But not now. He guessed she probably didn't like to talk about it. He understood that. There were many things he didn't like to talk about.

Later, they walked home. Holly chatted a lot. She skipped along the pathway and waved to people she knew.

"Mom will speak to the principal at our school. You'll be a sensation. We've never had anyone at school without a memory. Do you remember how to add up and how to write stories and how to spell and things that happened in history like the First Fleet?"

"I remember that most teachers are painful,

that I hate math and that the convicts had an awful time coming out to Australia and that a lot of them died. The ship stank and the food was half-rotten and there was never enough of it. The convicts got whipped when they complained and sometimes when they didn't. There were kids as young as nine on the ship. Sometimes you were chained to someone who died. Maybe it was someone you liked. Another kid. You woke up and he was lying there on the hammock beside you. White as chalk and frozen in time. Nobody cried. Not because they didn't care but because it was happening all the time. They would unchain him and toss him over the side of the boat." Daniel stopped. His lower lip was quivering. He bit it quickly, controlling himself.

"Hey, stop it. You're making it sound like you were there. You're spooking me out, Daniel. Here, we're home. I can smell, let's see, roast potatoes and roast beef and gardenias beside the veranda posts and roses and carnations."

"That sounds like a great dinner."

He watched as sunlight caught her hair. He thought of ravens' wings and midnight darkness, and moonlight streaking the ocean.

She saw him looking and he felt her . . . what? Confusion. Anger. Her cheeks flushed.

What had he done?

He turned away.

"Your mom's great."

"I know."

Chapter 5

The social worker, John, came to see him.

"It's odd," he said to Daniel, "nobody's reported you missing. Don't you remember anything?"

"No," said Daniel. "Not a thing. But I can stay here, can't I?"

"Yes, for the time being," the social worker said. "We've been to court to get a temporary order. All that means is that you're not to worry and you can stay put for now. Daniel, think. Don't you remember anything? Anything at all that would maybe give us a clue?"

"No," said Daniel patiently. He looked over to where Holly sat at a desk in the living room doing her homework. He could hear Sally in the kitchen bustling around. The wind chimes sang outside the front door. He felt peaceful. More peaceful than at Grandma's, more peaceful than with the elderly couple at the house in the country, where the sun sank beneath the horizon in a bright flame at the end of every day. More peaceful than in the small apartment near the water where he went to sleep with the sound of waves rolling gently onto the shoreline.

Daniel didn't want to leave this place. He nudged the social worker's mind and put a thought there.

"Well, of course, I'll recommend that you stay here as long as you like," he said to Daniel. "Hmm, I feel there was something else I wanted to say. What was it?"

Sally walked in from the kitchen. She wiped her hands on her apron and smiled at John.

"You said on the phone you were thinking about putting Daniel on TV. That way someone somewhere might recognize him."

"Of course. Yes. That was it. Heavens, I have a sudden headache." He put a hand to his head.

"Can I make you a cup of tea?" asked Sally.

"No. I'll be going along now." John looked confused.

"The television interview? Are you going to arrange it?" asked Sally.

"What television interview?"

Sally blinked. The social worker patted Daniel absently on his head. He absently patted his own head too, and, without saying another word, picked up his briefcase and left.

"What was that all about?" Sally said, asking no one in particular. Then she rubbed her head too.

"I feel dizzy suddenly. Maybe I need that cup of tea. It's wonderful having you stay with us, Daniel."

Daniel smiled at her through his bright-blue eyes.

Holly looked up from her homework. She opened her mouth as if to speak but seemed to think better of it.

Daniel probed her mind. Jealousy? How come? Why would she be jealous of him? She had everything. *No one but Mom and me, and Dad when he comes back,* he read in her mind.

He'd have to be careful. He liked this house. He liked Sally and he liked Holly too. He prodded her mind a little more deeply. Something else was troubling her but he couldn't make it out. He withdrew, deciding he wouldn't probe her mind too deeply. It gave people headaches and he liked his new family.

He wondered about school. They'd be going

there tomorrow. Sally had taken him out this morning to buy clothing and a school uniform. "I'm sure that your parents will turn up soon, but until then, well, you've got to go to school."

"Isn't all this stuff costing you heaps?"

"The social worker will make sure that I'm paid back," she laughed at him. She pointed around the store. "Look around you. Do you see anything, anything at all that strikes a chord, gives you a clue."

He dutifully stared around at the bright shops, the arcades, the busy streets. "No," he said. "Not a thing."

Daniel lay in bed that night, staring out through the open window at the stars and pale moon. He wondered what was up there. Whether people lived and worked and played on other planets far away. Whether they might look like him or maybe resemble some weird sea creature.

He wondered also whether there was anyone else on Earth like him. Everyone grew old; but not him.

Had he really been cursed to wander the Earth forever? Why? What had he done? Trodden on the foot of a demented wizard two hundred years ago?

The next day after breakfast, he and Holly walked to school. They reached a busy intersection where Holly met another girl.

"This is Daniel. Daniel, this is Angie." Daniel smiled at Angie, a fair-haired, freckle-faced girl who smiled shyly back.

"Holly told me you've lost your memory."

Daniel nodded.

"Everyone talks to him about that," said Holly. "I'm sure that any day now he'll remember who he is and his parents will come and take him home again."

He nudged her mind and felt relief coming

from her as she said this. This isn't good, he thought.

He could give her thoughts a push. Just a small one. She'd only get a tiny headache. He could make her like him. He hesitated. Suddenly it seemed important to be liked for himself. She was his age. Was he so awful? It would be good to be liked for himself. He'd take the chance. If things got difficult he could do what he always did—leave.

"You're right, Holly," he said and he kicked a small pebble on the sidewalk. "I think I'll get my memory back soon and then I'll be gone."

Holly blushed. She lowered her eyes and stared at the pavement, then faced him. A frown curled between her eyes. "I didn't really mean that I wanted you to go," she said.

He met the other kids in the class at the playground. Melanie, a small girl with red hair.

Ben, a tall stocky boy with grey eyes and spiky brown hair. He met others. Holly did not seem close to any of the other kids. He sensed discomfort, particularly with Ben. She stood well back from him.

"Why don't you like him?" he asked her as they lined up at the cafeteria.

"How do you know I don't like him?" Holly turned and stared at him. "Daniel, you're giving me the creeps. It's as if you can read my mind."

"I'm just, um, a good guesser," said Daniel.

"Ben makes fun of anyone who's different. That's why I don't like him."

"Well, he'll have a good time with me then."

"Not as much fun as he has with me," said Holly.

She turned away from him and he nudged her mind gently. It was like trying to put a fist through a brick wall. He could probe further but he'd have to give her a major headache to find out what was bothering her. No, he'd promised himself he wouldn't do this with Holly.

He filed into class with the others. The teacher made him stand up front like a nerd while she introduced him. "Daniel is staying with us for the time being," she told the class. "So be kind and friendly."

After school he walked with Angie and Holly to the gates. He listened while the girls talked together about movie stars and going to the beach, other kids and homework.

Ben sauntered past them. He turned around. "How's the freak doing?" he called out.

"I'm not a freak," Daniel and Holly shouted together; just like two parrots.

"Hey, you two make a great couple," Ben called back at them. "He's got no memory and you've got no . . ."

"Shut up, you creep," Angie called out.

Ben poked his tongue out at them. Swinging his school bag over one shoulder, he leapt over the school fence. He missed his footing and landed heavily on the earth on the other side. Daniel and Angie laughed.

"He's a big bully," said Holly.

"I know why he'd have a go at me," said Daniel. "But why you?"

Then he remembered. She didn't have eyelashes or eyebrows. "Sorry," he said. "Were you born without eyelashes and eyebrows?"

"Huh?" Holly got this vague look on her face. "Oh, that. Hmm. Yeah."

"Don't you start with her," Angie said protectively.

"I'm not. I wouldn't," said Daniel.

They walked along the street. Past shops and houses. Suddenly Ben leapt out from an alleyway between two shops. He jumped in front of Holly and pulled hard at her dark hair.

Daniel immediately rushed forward to push him away. Holly began to scream. Angie swung at Ben with her school bag.

"Get away from her."

It came off. Holly's hair. Ben had yanked a wig from her head. Now he held it triumphantly in his hand while Holly stood there, her head as bald as an egg. Tears stung her eyes. She couldn't say a word.

While Angie and Daniel grappled with Ben, he quickly tossed the wig away. It flew through the air, was caught up in a sudden windy gust, and landed on the road. It looked like some furry creature. A truck swerved to miss it. The car behind couldn't avoid the wig and drove right over it. Holly in the meantime had curled up on the pavement, putting her hands protectively over her scalp.

Ben, who was taller and stronger than Angie and Daniel, easily pushed them away. He ran off.

"Bye bye, freaks," he yelled at them.

"I'm the only freak around here," Holly muttered miserably as Angie pulled her to her feet.

"Don't pay attention to Ben. He's nuts," Angie said.

"And you, you can just stop looking at me," Holly said to Daniel. "Haven't you ever seen a bald twelve-year-old girl before? Well, I s'pose not."

Daniel didn't answer. He ran on to the road and picked up the wig. It was dirty and the inside of it had been torn by the car's impact. He shook some of the dirt out of it and ran back to the pavement.

"Here," he said to Holly. "I'd never laugh at you." His cheeks grew hot. "I still think you're pretty."

"Oh yeah, really," said Holly sullenly. She put the wig back on her head, even though it was torn. Passers-by stared at her.

"Let's get out of here," Angie said.

They crossed the road and Angie said goodbye.

"Don't let that creep Ben make you feel bad about yourself."

Holly didn't reply. She nodded stiffly, continuing along the street. Then her walk turned into a run. Daniel had trouble keeping up with her.

"Slow down, Holly."

"I hate myself," Holly said to him. "I hate the way I was born without eyelashes or eyebrows or hair. I hate being different."

"Me too," said Daniel.

"You're not different. At least you don't look different. You'll get your memory back. You'll go back to live with your parents and the only memory that will go will be the time you spent with us."

"That's not true. Anyway you're not the only one with a secret."

She stopped running and looked curiously at him. "So you do remember something. You do, don't you?"

Daniel fumbled for words. "Not exactly, not really. It's just that . . ."

"And you always seem to know what I'm thinking or feeling. What's that about?"

"It's the way I am," said Daniel quietly.

Holly walked up the sidewalk. "I have another wig," she said. "It's just like this one." She added, "I don't care any more that you know. Everyone at school knows. You'd have found out sooner or later. One day when I was little, the wind blew my new wig away. It was a loose fit. The wig was blown all around the playground and the kids laughed."

Sally was upset about what had happened to Holly. "I'm going to phone the school tomorrow and get the phone number of that boy's parents."

"Mom, don't. Just don't. It will make it worse for me at school."

"I'm going to anyway. You just can't let kids act like that."

Sally shook her head angrily. She began to peel potatoes. "Here, Daniel," she said. "Cut up some fruit for dessert."

Daniel sat in the kitchen. He diced pieces of orange and apple, and took chops out of the fridge. Soon there was the comforting smell of dinner cooking.

"I really like being here," Daniel said over dinner.

"And we like having you here," said Sally.

Daniel probed her mind. He smiled. She meant it. She was happy he was there.

Later, after Holly and he had finished their homework, after he'd showered and gone to bed, Daniel lay in his bed and thought to himself: *It would be great if I could help Holly. If I could get her hair to grow again. I can nudge brains and make people think things they wouldn't think about otherwise. I've never really tried to make someone's body different.*

So he concentrated. He imagined Holly's scalp covered with tiny dark hair that grew and grew. He thought about her eyes and imagined her with long thick eyelashes as dark as midnight. He thought of her eyebrows. He imagined small shafts of hair sprouting and forming a delicate curve above her eyes.

He fell asleep, forgetting about Holly, and instead saw strange creatures with skinny arms and legs and pointed faces and eyes that had no lids. They flew around him, arms linked, whispering to him, "We're coming, we'll soon be there." He felt his feet lift off from the ground as he flew with them. Over meadows and farms and large cities, and high above the earth until it was just a swirling blue–green planet far below.

Chapter 6

The weeks flew by. Daniel went to school with Holly and Angie and, though he didn't make other close friends in the class, it didn't seem to matter.

He kept well away from Ben. Sally had spoken to Ben's parents and Ben had snarled at them but left them alone.

On the weekends Daniel went to the movies or the beach with Holly and Angie. Once he'd played football with them and some other kids from his class.

Sally kissed him every night before he went to

bed and Holly felt so comfortable with him that she'd walk around the house without her wig on.

The social worker didn't come again. Sally sometimes asked about his memory coming back, but not often. Daniel had seen to that.

He began to feel contented. *I'll stay here just as long as I can. For years and years. Until they look at me in that strange, curious way. Until others notice.*

One night Sally said to Holly and Daniel, "I'm going out for dinner. It's still light outside and I'll only be gone about two hours so I figure you kids are fine by yourselves. Just don't let anyone in the house."

She added, "I'm having dinner with Michael."

Holly bit her lip.

When Sally went to the bedroom to change, Daniel asked Holly, "What's up? How come you don't want your mom to go out."

"She's going out with the guy who owns the pet shop where she works," she said. "I know she likes him a lot. She used to date him before you came to stay with us. He's been overseas and now he's back. What if he likes her too? I mean, if he *really* likes her."

"Why is that a problem?"

"Well, maybe they'll marry, my dad will never come back, and my mom will care more about him than me."

"Hang on, that's crazy. She's just going out for dinner with him."

"And wait till he finds out his future stepdaughter's bald," said Sally, stroking her shiny head.

"And that his future stepson has no memory," said Daniel. He laughed nervously. Maybe he'd gone too far in hinting that he considered himself part of the family. But Holly either didn't notice or care and she giggled too.

Later, when Sally was ready to leave, Daniel could see that her dark hair had been newly cut and her eyes sparkled. She wore a red dress that clung to her and made her look, well, pretty cool.

"Have a good time," Daniel said to Sally. She reached down to him and kissed him on the cheek.

Holly held back a little. She stared up at her mother and whispered, "Come home real soon."

Her mother hugged her. When Holly closed the door behind her, she said to Daniel, "I sometimes miss my dad."

"You look like him," Daniel said.

Holly frowned. "You're doing it again. How do you know I look like him?"

Daniel licked his lips nervously. He had never, in all these years, wanted to tell someone about himself the way he did now.

"You read minds," Holly continued. "You do

things with your head. I know. I've seen you at school too. You pretend sometimes not to know the right answer, but I can tell. You know everything before the teacher teaches it. I even caught you once writing down the correct answer to something, then crossing it out as though you didn't want to be too clever. Also, how come, after all this time, no one's come to get you? Even the social worker doesn't come. And your picture was never on television. What's going on?"

She stood there, her arms folded, waiting for an answer. Daniel wondered then whether he should have nudged her mind weeks ago into accepting him. He was about to reply when he noticed something.

Could it be? *No.*

Was it possible? *Maybe.*

Just maybe.

"Holly, feel the top of your head."

"Why? Has a bird landed on it?"

"Don't joke. Just do it."

She put her hand on the top of her scalp, then squealed.

"I don't believe it," she said. She raced to the mirror in the lounge room. She screamed, "Hair. I'm getting hair."

Daniel sat there smiling. He'd done it. He'd done this crazy, wonderful thing.

She pushed her face right up to the mirror. "I can't believe it. Eyebrows and eyelashes. They're tiny, almost invisible, but they're there. What's happened to me?"

Daniel felt happier than he'd ever felt before. Holly ran around the room hopping up and down. She continually touched the fine down of hair covering her head. "Wait till Mom sees this."

Then she stopped in her tracks. "Maybe it's just for now. Maybe by tomorrow the hair will have dropped out."

"No," said Daniel. He shook his head firmly. "It won't. It's going to stay. I just know it."

Holly ran from mirror to mirror. "Hair, I'm getting hair. This doesn't seem real. Why has it happened now?"

She yelled out to him from her bedroom, "I'll have to tell Angie. Tomorrow I'm going to buy myself a comb and a brush and hair shampoo and conditioner."

She ran back to the living room. Then she stopped still in her tracks and stared at Daniel, where he sat smiling at her on the sofa. She sat by him and calmly said, "What do you have to do with this, Daniel?"

"Nothing," he said and he waved his hands in front of him.

"That's not true," said Holly "There's something you're not telling me. Why? It can't be that bad. Are you in trouble?"

"No, not really," said Daniel. He tapped a finger nervously on the side of the sofa.

"Come on, then," said Holly. "You can trust me. I won't tell anyone. Not even myself. Honest."

The blue of his eyes seemed to deepen. He would tell her. He would. She wouldn't believe him but he'd tell her anyway.

I feel like I've been bound and gagged forever. My first dad told me never to tell, that people wouldn't understand. And I haven't told. I've just moved on when people have become too curious. But Holly's different. She's had her own worries; she's more understanding. She's a kid, like me, even if I've been a kid for hundreds of years. I want to tell her. I want to . . .

So he did.

Chapter 7

He spoke for what seemed ages. He told Holly about the Scottish farmer, the time in London begging on the streets, coming out to Australia on a stinking, convict-filled ship, of Joe who took him in. He spoke of some of the many families he'd stayed with. The couple in the country where he'd helped milk cows early in the morning before he went to school. How one day, when he'd been there five years, four men had turned up at the farm and tried to kidnap him. Word had spread about the boy who did not grow up, and they had some idea that, if they kidnapped him, he'd tell them his secret of staying forever young.

All the time Holly sat cross-legged on the carpet in front of him. Her dark eyes widened and her mouth opened a little as she listened to him.

Daniel felt a huge surge of relief as he spoke about himself. His blue eyes darted from side to side as he remembered. Words came tumbling out. At times his speech changed. For instance, when he spoke about Scotland he used words like "ye" and "lad" and Holly blinked a few times at that.

"And so I nudge people I like, Holly, so that they will take me in."

Holly shook her head several times as if trying to shake away the impossible stories he was telling. But just when she'd decided that it couldn't be true, she reached up and felt her scalp. She stroked the soft down covering it and touched the buds of hair growing on her eyelids, where one day there'd be normal eyelashes.

"So you sort of nudged my mom, did you?"

"Yes. I know it sounds weird, maybe awful too, but I don't know what else I can do. Yes, I'm hundreds of years old, but I'm still a kid. I still think like a kid. If I just roam the streets, I get picked up by the police. I need to have a home."

"And me? Did you nudge my mind too?"

Daniel's face grew red then. He saw that she looked anxious. Angry maybe?

"A little. Then I stopped."

"Why?"

"I've never stayed in a home where there was a child. Every time I've gone to school I've been picked on. I haven't particularly liked the kids I've met. You're the first."

"Why couldn't you nudge the minds of the kids at school so they didn't pick on you?"

"Sometimes I did that, but it's not much fun forcing kids to like you. With you, I don't know why, it was important that you liked me for myself."

"And the social worker who doesn't come any more ...?"

"Yes, I fixed that."

"My hair?"

"I've never tried that before. I didn't know I could do it. I concentrated really hard and it just happened. I don't know why."

Holly clasped her hands together. She shivered though it was warm. She didn't say anything for ages as she tried to make sense of it all.

Finally she stood up. She looked seriously at him. "I believe you. I feel weird when I think that you nudge people's minds. It's awesome that you've got that power. I love that you fixed my hair. Don't you ever wonder—why you? Why you turned out different from everyone else?"

"I wonder all the time. I'd love to get older. I'd love to be able to talk about what I'm going to do when I grow up. But I'm never going to grow up."

"That's sad." Holly thought briefly about what she wanted to do. How she'd like to be a reporter or maybe a scientist. How, when she was younger, she wanted to be a train driver. Her choices had changed as she'd grown.

"If you could grow up, what would you want to be?"

"I'm not going to grow up. I can't think about the future. The future for me is forever wandering the world as a child."

Just then they both heard the front door open. "It's only me. I've brought Michael home."

Holly made a face. "I hate him." She ran to her bedroom and came out wearing her wig. Her eyelashes and eyebrows were too faint to be picked up by her mother. She'd show her later.

"Hi, Holly," the tall dark man said to Holly as she came out from her bedroom. He walked into the living room, smiling at Daniel as Sally introduced them.

"We had a great meal but we thought we'd have dessert right here," said Sally. "Spend time with you kids."

She went to the kitchen and began to rummage around in the fridge. Michael sat in an armchair. "I hear you've lost your memory, Daniel," he said. His eyes were crinkled at the sides and his smile was friendly.

"Yes," said Daniel. He felt a wave of anger coming from Holly. She really didn't like Michael.

"I went past your pet shop the other day," Daniel said to him. "Do you have any guinea pigs?"

"The ones I had used to fight all the time,"

Michael said. He turned to Holly. "How's it going, Holly?"

"Fine," said Holly, her voice clipped and distant. She sat at the far end of the sofa, her arms tightly folded.

"How's school?"

"Okay."

Michael coughed. He scratched his chin, then asked Daniel, "Do you ever get any flashes of memory?"

"No," said Daniel. He watched Holly. Why did she dislike Michael so much?

Sally came into the living room with a tray. "Here," she said. She gave Michael a thick slice of chocolate cake covered with cream. She gave the same to Holly and Daniel.

"This tastes great," said Daniel.

Holly ate quietly. She nibbled at the cake and looked unhappy. It made Daniel feel unhappy too.

She did that to him.

He made a decision.

He nudged Michael's mind. At first he met resistance. It was as if he was pushing against a door. Daniel pushed back. He gave the door a huge shove and suddenly he was there. Inside Michael's mind. He'd just do a little bit of doctoring with Michael's thoughts.

"This cake is awful," Michael said suddenly. He wiped his face with a napkin. "Don't you know I can't stand chocolate cake?"

"But you told me . . . ?" Sally said, her eyes widening in surprise.

"I'd better go home."

"Why? What's up?"

Michael stood up. "I'm tired."

He nodded stiffly at Daniel and Holly, and walked quickly to the front door. Sally came racing after him.

Holly and Daniel could hear a raised angry voice and a surprised response. The door closed and Sally came back into the living room looking confused.

"I don't know what that was all about," she said absently, more to herself than anyone else.

Holly said, "I've never liked him."

"Holly," said Sally, "don't say that. You're stuck with the idea that one day your dad and I are going to get back together. That's not going to happen. I like Michael very, very much. What happened then was completely out of character."

Daniel shifted awkwardly on the sofa.

Holly stared briefly at him, then suddenly remembered. She pulled off her wig. "Mom," she said excitedly. "Come here. Look! I'm growing hair. Eyebrows too and eyelashes."

"What?" Sally forgot Michael immediately. She ran to Holly and nervously touched the fine soft hair on her scalp. "It's not possible," she said.

She looked at her face, at the tiny eyelashes and the beginnings of eyebrows there. "How?" she asked.

"I don't know," Holly lied, "but isn't it wonderful? I'll be able to have a brush and comb just like other kids. And I'll have to buy shampoo . . ."

Sally put her arms around Holly. "I don't know what to say. I was told by the doctors that you'd never grow hair. It was just the way you were. This is a miracle."

"I guess it is," said Holly, looking at Daniel.

Chapter 8

Weeks went by. Holly's hair grew quickly. She stopped wearing her wig altogether and her short hair framed her face giving her a pixie-like appearance. Her eyelashes thickened and her eyebrows, just a light pencil-stroke before, were now like small dark wings.

"You spend a lot of time in front of the mirror now." Daniel smiled at her. "I can never get in the bathroom."

Angie came over.

"Angie, my hair's really wavy," said Holly.

"Look."

"Holly, *I know*. Can't you give it a rest," Angie sighed, as Holly sat brushing her hair.

"That's not fair," said Holly. "You don't know how it felt to be bald."

"Okay, and now you're not. So get used to it. You're no fun to be with," she said. "Daniel and I are going down the beach. Want to come?"

"There's this program on TV about hair-care. I *really* want to watch it. It's about hairstyles and conditioners and . . ."

"Oh, be quiet," said Angie. She turned to Daniel. "Get your swimsuit and let's get out of here."

Holly looked uptight. "Can't you wait until the program is over?"

"No, maybe it will be raining by then. I want to go out now. You're becoming boring."

Daniel looked at Holly. She had her arms folded and was staring angrily at Angie. He reached into

Angie's mind and gave it a nudge.

"Sure, I'd like to watch TV and find out about hairstyles and stuff," said Angie. "And then we can brush each other's hair and give each other different hairstyles. Yours is still a bit short but . . ."

Holly stared at her, then at Daniel. Daniel looked away. The girls sat in front of the TV and Angie oohed and aahed just as much as Holly at the different models and the amazing hairstyles. Daniel was bored silly. He got out a book to read.

Later, after Angie had gone home, Holly said, "Put that book down. We've got to talk."

He shut the book. "What's up?"

"You're giving me the creeps. That's what's up."

"What do you mean?"

"You know exactly what I mean. You nudged Angie's mind, didn't you?"

"Well, okay, yes. Why aren't you happy? You got what you wanted."

Holly stared away from him at some vague point on the opposite wall. She stared for a long time. "You've got to stop it. The nudging, I mean. You're messing with people's brains. I'd rather have an argument with Angie than have her do something she doesn't want to do. We'd get over an argument."

"It was just a dumb TV show. It's not like . . ."

"No, let me finish," said Holly. "Haven't you noticed how moody Mom is? She really liked Michael, and you and I messed that up. You did it for me but it's really my fault. I really did think that Mom and Dad might get back together if Michael wasn't in the picture. Now I see that Mom and Dad won't. That it's got nothing to do with Michael. Do you know that Mom's going to leave her job? She told me that it's too difficult working for Michael now. She's miserable."

"No, I didn't know that," said Daniel. He shook

his head. "I only wanted to help."

"Well, you've got to make things the way they were, Daniel, and then you've got to stop messing with people's brains. That means messing with my mom's brain as well. She likes you a lot. You don't have to nudge her into keeping you here. You've never really controlled my thinking and, though I find you a bit weird at times, you're like, well, my brother now."

Daniel felt confused. She was right. He'd never forced her to like him but she did anyway. It really did feel better to be liked for himself than by nudging her emotions.

"Okay," he said.

He went out for a walk later. Down to the pet shop. Sally went to the city in the van on Tuesday afternoons to buy bulk pet food.

Michael was in the shop by himself feeding the fish.

"Hi, Michael," Daniel said.

Michael turned around. He frowned ever so slightly. "Hi there, Daniel. How's the memory coming along?"

"Okay," said Daniel. He shrugged, and turned to look at a small puppy in a cage. He knelt and felt the soft paw. At the same time he reached right into Michael's mind. Opened the locked door. Took out the thought he'd placed there.

He looked up.

Michael shook himself as if he was suddenly throwing off a huge weight. "Phew," he said.

"Feeling better now?" Daniel asked him sheepishly.

"Yes, I am," said Michael. "What made you ask?"

"Well, um, you haven't smiled in a while and you're smiling now."

Daniel left Michael whistling to himself. He'll be okay now, thought Daniel. When Sally comes back he'll say how sorry he is that he's been so moody. She'll stay working at the shop and one day maybe they'll fall in love.

He met Angie at the shops. "I'm going to the drugstore. My mom thinks I've gone nuts," she told him. "I'm spending all my pocket money on hair conditioners and hair mousse. I don't even know why I'm doing it."

He felt the conflict in her mind and removed it. She sighed deeply. "Maybe I'll buy a comic instead."

Daniel went home. Now for Sally. He'd remove the nudge. This was the biggest chance he'd taken so far.

Holly and he peeled vegetables and put on a roast. They'd make a great meal for Sally.

Later, when the house was filled with good cooking smells, Sally opened the front door. "What's that I smell?"

She walked into the kitchen, her nose twitching. "Wow. You're cooking dinner?"

Holly smiled. "Mom, why don't you give Michael a call? Maybe ask him over to eat with us?"

"Oh no," said Sally. "I dropped off the pet food at the shop and didn't even stop to talk to him. He's been impossible."

"He's, um, had a few problems," said Daniel. "I went in there today. He's his old self, honest."

"Pleeeeease," said Holly.

Sally felt confused. While she stood there, trying to decide, Daniel quietly slithered into her mind. He removed the nudge. It was risky.

"Okay," laughed Sally. "Daniel, give him a call, seeing as you're so sure he's snapped out of his rotten mood."

Then she looked suddenly at Daniel and blinked a few times. *It's as if she's seeing me for the first time, thought Daniel.*

"You know if your parents ever turn up, I don't know how I'm going to let you go, Daniel," she said. "Promise me that even if you do get your memory back and leave us that you'll always feel we're part of your family."

He ran to her and hugged her.

Chapter 9

"If your parents don't claim you, I'm going to adopt you," said Sally to Daniel one day and she ruffled his hair. "How do you feel about that?"

"Great. I feel great."

Six months had passed. Holly and he were closer than ever, though they had the usual sister–brother fights from time to time. Holly's hair had grown thick and lustrous, though no one had been able to explain how it had happened.

The social worker, John, visited regularly. However, there were certain things that Daniel wouldn't undo. The nudge he'd given people who had given him a home in the past stayed. It was kinder for them that they believed he had been taken back by his real parents and that their memory of him dimmed with the passing years.

He went to school with Holly and Angie and slowly started to make other friends there. He stopped peeking into other kids' thoughts.

Michael came round to the house regularly. He took the family to the movies and became coach of the local soccer team. Daniel and Holly played at the soccer field each Saturday afternoon. Daniel, slow at first and unsure of the rules, began to score goals.

Only Holly knew Daniel's secret. Daniel began to feel so much at home that he buried that secret deep inside of him. He wasn't going to worry about the years to come. Not for a long, long time.

Daniel felt the prodding in his head one night as he was curled up in bed reading. He'd just reached a part in the book where the main character was climbing a mountain when he was caught in an avalanche. Suddenly Daniel felt something crawling around inside his head. He heard words too. Strange words that he didn't understand at first . . .

Daniel put the book down. What was happening? He cupped both hands over his ears. The voices were becoming louder.

"Estram, we're back. Sorry it took so long."

"He doesn't remember a thing. Remember, we blanked out his memories. He's not responding."

"Keep our voices down. His human ears are aching."

"He's becoming upset."

"He doesn't know what is happening."

"Shall we give him his memory back?"

"Estram, do you hear us?"

Estram? The name flickered like a dull light through his mind. It sounded awfully familiar.

"Estram, we didn't realize we'd been gone so long in Earth time."

"We're going now. You'll start to remember a few things over the next few Earth days, then we'll pick you up."

"Take you home."

"To Syzomp."

"Remember?"

"It's all too much for him."

Daniel thought he was going crazy. He felt the voices fly around his head like a flock of birds. *Many parts; one mind.* That flickered through his thoughts. *"You can't take me home, I am home,"* he answered.

"You'll start to remember. We'll be back. Sleep now."

Daniel leaned back on his bed. His eyes closed,

his eyelids twitching as he dreamed about swirling people with silver bodies and linked arms. *Many parts, one mind,* he heard the voice say. *Estram,* he heard them call.

When he awoke his head throbbed.

"Wow, I had such a weird dream," he said to Holly as they walked to school.

"Me too. I dreamt I was stuck in a lift with Ben. And he was gassy at the time."

"Yuck. I dreamt that my real name was Estram and that I was from some other place. An alien world called Syzomp. These alien guys were telling me that they were coming for me. They were in my mind. It felt so real. They said they were sorry they'd left me on Earth for so long. The freaky thing is that the name 'Estram' sounded familiar. And so did the name of the alien world."

Holly stopped walking. She bit her lip then said,

"Daniel, are you *sure*, I mean *really sure*, that you had a dream?"

"Sure I'm sure. What else could it have been?"

Holly frowned. "I don't know."

Later in the day he began to feel it. Threads of distant memory linking together like a patchwork quilt. But was it a memory? It seemed to come from so long ago.

A planet. Two suns—one each side of the sky giving the sky its apricot color. Pink soil. Plants that reached up to the sky. People—were they people?—floating around. Their long silver arms were linked. They were like birds that suddenly turned together to fly as if there was one mind directing them.

No homes—just floating beings occasionally resting on the tall branches of the plants, whose top branches nestled in pearly clouds. There was no sense of time here. Just thought. No families.

Only linked arms and silver bodies and a buzzing mind made up of many minds.

I separated from the others, he thought. *We landed on Earth. A scientific expedition, they said. But something went wrong. I was hurt. I became detached from the Whole. They tried to pull me back to them but I was apart. They couldn't do it.*

Daniel blinked and tried to push these thoughts from his mind. He wasn't sure what was happening. He didn't like to believe that these thoughts were distant memories. Glimmers of light from the distant past.

After school Angie, Holly and he went to the shops. They slurped on popsicles.

When Angie left them at the corner to go to her house, Daniel nervously said, "I don't think I had a dream last night, Holly. Someone, something is nudging my mind. I'm getting thoughts. Memories maybe."

He told Holly everything. "If they really are memories, then they're getting ready to take me back."

"Does that mean you'll be leaving us, your family?"

"I don't know. I just have this creepy feeling that someone, something's coming for me."

Chapter  10

It was early evening. Michael and Sally were out walking.

Holly and Daniel were playing a board game. Daniel suddenly tipped up the game and put both hands against the side of his head.

"They're here," he said. "In my mind."

Holly watched him anxiously.

Eventually he turned to her. His eyes, piercing blue, had a strange fire in them.

"Daniel?" Holly asked. "What's happening?"

"I remember," he said. "I remember it all."

Daniel leaned against the back of the chair. The blue of his eyes deepened. "My name is Estram. Our name is Estram. I am part of the Whole. We are not individual people like on Earth. We are many bodies with just one mind. Our thoughts are connected. We came to Earth as scientists and explorers, like the old-time explorers who set sail on Earth. The universe is like a vast sea filled with amazing places."

"Our world is beautiful like Earth but so different. We have no sense of time. We just exist. We float in the thin air between pink clouds and at night we drift in the night sky between the six moons of our planet. We have no need of food. Nor do we harm other creatures. We are a peaceful Whole. We came to Earth in a swirling mass of cloud that cuts through time and space. But there was a terrible storm and the cloud separated. I was injured and grew apart from the others.

"They had to leave me here. They would be back with a link from our planet, they said, so I could rejoin them. I could not survive without the others. So they gave me an Earth body. That of a child. They thought that would be safe. Unfortunately, when they gave me an Earth body, my own memories went. They left me with powers—powers that came from my planet—but no memory of who I was. I didn't age because the body was of a twelve-year-old. It wasn't meant to get older. They'd be back soon, they told me."

"Over two hundred years isn't exactly soon," commented Holly.

"There is no understanding of time on my planet as it exists on Earth. A mistake was made," said Daniel. "This is what they are telling me now."

He paused, listening to voices in his mind.

"They are asking me where they should meet

me, to link me up again to the Whole."

"And what are you going to tell them, Daniel?"asked Holly softly.

"I don't want to go."

"Will they give you a choice?"

He crept out of bed and into the back garden that night. They'd told him all the coordinates had been worked out. I don't want to go home, he'd said. But you are part of the Whole, they'd replied. You belong with us. When you see us, you will want to rejoin us.

Daniel woke Holly. Together they stood in the back garden, frightened and excited.

The sky was a twinkling sea of stars. The moon a lopsided boomerang

They waited while the trees rustled and the branches moved like pointed fingers.

A swirling pink cloud appeared above them.

From the middle of it, strange people, all linking hands, silver beings with long spindly arms and spindly legs floated to the ground. They had lidless eyes, small squat noses and no mouths.

They don't eat, thought Holly. Not even chocolate.

They stood on the grass, facing Daniel and Holly.

They talked to Daniel in his mind. "We are here," they said. "We are ready for you to rejoin the Whole."

"Talk in Earth-talk," Daniel said to them in his mind. "She is my friend. She can't hear you."

"A friend. Ah yes, we understand," they said. This time Holly heard them, a low-pitched voice that seemed to come from all of them.

"I don't want to go back," said Daniel. "Over two hundred Earth years have gone by. This is a long time. I remember my old world and how I was part of the Whole. But on Earth it is different.

Here I am just one person who has wandered a lonely path. Now I am with a family I have grown to care for."

"Care for? Ah, the Earth family. Different from ours. But you must rejoin the Whole."

"I don't want to," protested Daniel.

Their voices rose. They talked together, argued with one another. They held out their linked hands to Daniel. "Rejoin," they said as one.

"No," said Daniel.

Their bodies shimmered, faded, then became bright silver again.

"If you stay, we must leave you forever. You shall grow older. You shall not have the powers that we left you with to protect you."

"That's cool," said Daniel.

"*Cool*. Hmm, an Earth expression for pleasure," they nodded at him. "Are you very sure? We shall not come back."

"I'm sure."

They spoke again to one another. Many voices arguing. At last they floated back to the pink cloud.

The cloud hovered above a tree before it abruptly disappeared.

Chapter

In the morning Sally had trouble getting the children up for breakfast. "I'm tired," complained Daniel.

"Let me sleep in," said Holly.

Daniel eventually got up. He showered and put on his T-shirt and shorts. He stared at himself in the mirror. At the bright-blue eyes, the red-brown hair. He looked a little closer.

He gave a squeal. Holly came rushing into his room. "What is it?"

"A pimple. I've got my first pimple."

Holly grinned.

I can make plans, Daniel thought. One day I'll be grown up and I'll become a . . . well, I don't know what I want to become when I grow up.

I'll have to give that some thought. He stroked the pimple.

After all, I'm getting older.

About Moya Simons

Once, I was in a classroom where most of the children were about eleven or twelve. We began to talk about getting older and discussed how great it would be to stay young forever. Most of the children thought eighteen would be a fine age to stay forever—when they were officially adults but still teenagers.

However, one child said, "I'd like to be twelve-years-old forever. I love being twelve. Being a kid is great."

I began to think about this after I left the school. How would it be if you stayed, say, twelve? How would you go about getting work? How about never growing up and having your own children? What about people who might view you with suspicion and even jealousy? You'd have to keep moving on and how sad it would be to have people you loved eventually grow old and die.

This finally gave rise to this book, *The Boy Who Would Live Forever.*

All writers know that ideas come from many sources. Sometimes, it's an unusual face in a train. Other times a story is inspired by a person you've just met. On this occasion it was a chance remark from a child. He wanted to stay twelve-years-old, to be *The Boy Who Would Live Forever.*